# SMACK DAB
## IN THE MIDDLE

written & illustrated by

### Anita Riggio

G. P. Putnam's Sons        New York

Library of Congress Cataloging-in-Publication Data
Riggio, Anita. Smack dab in the middle / Anita Riggio. p. cm. Summary: Rosie is happy to be smack dab in the middle of her large family, but sometimes she feels neglected or ignored. [1. Family life—Fiction.] I. Title. PZ7.R44187 Sm 2002 [E]—dc21 00-066472   ISBN 0-399-23700-3
10 9 8 7 6 5 4 3 2 1   First Impression

Thanks to my mentors and friends
at Vermont College,
who helped me "go there."
Thanks to Bill Reiss,
who noticed a time warp.
Thanks to Kathy Dawson,
who loved Rosie at first sight.

For my family —
who else? —
with love.

Rosie Roselli had a mother and a father, a sister and a brother, a grandma and a grandpa, a *nonna* and a *nonno*, four aunts and four uncles, and twelve cousins—six older and six younger. And Rosie Roselli was smack dab in the middle of them all.

One morning, her teacher, Sister Celestia, said,
"Counting time, Friends! Today we count
the people in our families."
"Yes, Sister!" said the Friends.
Rosie Roselli cracked her knuckles.
She drummed her fingers.
Then she selected one bead for each person
in her family. When all the beads were
lined up in a row, she counted them.
Twenty-nine, thought Rosie Roselli.
I counted twenty-nine people in my family.
Rosie bloomed.

"Oh my, Rosie Roselli," Sister Celestia said,
"what a big bead family you have."
"This is me," Rosie said, pointing to the pink bead
in the center of the bunch. "Smack dab in the middle."
"Smack dab in the middle seems to suit you,
Rosie Roselli. This is Good Work," Sister Celestia said.
"You deserve a star."
"Thank you, Sister."
That afternoon, Rosie raced
home from school.

"Look at this, everybody!"
she yelled.
"Look at my Good Work!"

"A little later, Rosie dear,"
said her uncle.
"I have to teach your big cousin
to drive the car."

"A little later, Rosie darling,"
said her aunt.
"I have to tuck your little cousin
in for a nap."

Rosie Roselli stuck her paper on the refrigerator with two magnets.

She waited for her big cousin to be taught.

She waited for her little cousin to be tucked.

She waited.

And waited.

But no one came back to look.

Rosie Roselli drooped.

The next day, Sister Celestia asked, "Friends,
did your families like your Good Work?"
"Yes, Sister!" said the Friends.
But not Rosie Roselli.
"Hmmm," said Sister Celestia.
She opened the Music Cupboard.
"Music time, Friends.
Today we strike up the band!"
"Yes, Sister!" said the Friends.
Sister Celestia gave out drums
and cymbals and flutes.
She gave Rosie Roselli a bright red horn.

Rosie Roselli set her feet apart just so.
She put her horn to her lips.
*Pppff.*
Rosie Roselli rolled her shoulders.
She stretched her neck from side to side.
She tried again.
*Bbeeh.*
And again.
*BbbbeeeeeEEEHHHHHHHH!!!!!!!!!!*
Rosie Roselli beamed.

"Friends," Sister Celestia called out,
"everybody follow our leader, Rosie Roselli."
And Rosie led the Friends THRUMM-THRUMMing
and KKSSSHH-KKSSSHHing
and BBEEEHH-BBEEEHHing
all around the room.
That afternoon,
Rosie zoomed home
from school.

"Listen to this!"

"*Un momento*, Rosie dear,"
said her nonna.
"I have to help your
little cousin."

"*Un momento*, Rosie darling,"
said her nonno. "I have to cart your
big cousins to Boy Scouts."

Rosie waited for her little cousin to be helped.
She waited for her big cousins to be carted.
She waited.
And waited.
But no one came back to listen.
Rosie Roselli paled.

The next day, Sister Celestia asked,
"Friends, did your families like your Music?"
"Yes, Sister!" said the Friends.
But not Rosie Roselli.
"Hmmm," said Sister Celestia.
She clapped her hands.
"Creative Movement time, Friends.
Feel the tempo in your feet!"
"Yes, Sister!" said the Friends.

Sister Celestia sat down
at the upright piano.
"Roll out the barrels," Sister sang.
"We'll have a barrel of fun."
The tempo tickled Rosie's toes.
She tapped her foot.

"Roll out the barrels,
     we've got the blues on the run!"
Tempo seeped up through the soles
     of Rosie's saddle shoes.
Rosie Roselli rose up on her toes.
"Zing! Boom! Tar-ra-ra!" the Friends sang.
"Sing out the song with good cheer!"
Tempo tickled. Tempo prickled.

"Now's the time to roll out
the barrels 'cause the gang's all here!"
Tem-po *de-lish-i-o*! Tem-po *ir-re-sis-ti-bo*!
Rosie Roselli flung her arms wide,
grabbed that tempo, and twirled with gusto!
That afternoon, Rosie dashed home from school.

"Watch this!"

"A little later, Rosie dear,"
said her father.
"After I help your brother
with his homework."

"A little later, Rosie darling,"
said her mother.
"After I soothe your sister."

Rosie whined.
She wailed.
She sighed.
What about me? Rosie wondered.

Rosie Roselli
really needed a hug.
She needed a hug
right this minute,
but her mother's arms
were full of Rosie's sister.
Rosie Roselli couldn't wait.
She stepped up close.
She breathed in.
Talcum powder
and lavender water.
It smelled like a hug.
But it didn't feel
like one.
Then and there,
Rosie Roselli decided
just what she
must do.

The next day, Sister Celestia asked,
"Friends, did your families
like your Creative Movements?"
"Yes, Sister!" said the Friends.
But not Rosie Roselli.
"Hmmm," said Sister Celestia.
She tied on her apron.
"Art time, Friends!
Today we draw Family Portraits."
"Yes, Sister!" said the Friends.

Rosie selected a bouquet of chubby crayons.
She drew:
a mother and a father,
a sister and a brother,
a grandma and a grandpa,
a nonna and a nonno,
four aunts and four uncles,
and twelve cousins—
six older and six younger.
Then Rosie drew herself
smack dab in the middle
of them all.

"Oh my, Rosie Roselli," Sister Celestia said. "There are lots of people who love you."

"Only sometimes, Sister. This is me," said Rosie, pointing to the teensy-weensiest person in the center of the paper. "Smack dab in the middle."

"It's a fine portrait."

"Thank you, Sister. It will remind me of my family when I run away."

"You plan to run away, Rosie Roselli?"

"Yes, Sister," said Rosie, "but nobody will notice."

"I see . . . " said Sister Celestia.

"I'm running away with my Good Work, my bright red horn, and tempo in my toes."

"And why is that?"

"Because they remind me of me," Rosie replied.

"It is wise to bear in mind who you are, Rosie Roselli," said Sister Celestia.

"Would you be able to do your homework before you go?"

"I guess so, Sister."

"Very well, then," Sister Celestia said. "Please ask every person in your family to sign the back of your Family Portrait."

"Yes, Sister," Rosie replied.

Then she headed home.

"I'm running away," Rosie Roselli told her mother and father and her sister and brother. "But before I go, please sign my Family Portrait."

"I'm running away," Rosie Roselli told her grandma and grandpa and her nonna and nonno. "But before I go, please sign my Family Portrait."

"I'm running away," Rosie Roselli told her aunts and uncles and all twelve
of her cousins. "But before I go, please sign my Family Portrait."
They all signed Rosie's Family Portrait. But not before each one
took a good long look at the teensy-weensiest person
smack dab in the middle of the picture.

"Rosie darling, you're not
teensy-weensy to us.
We love you,"
said her mother and father.
"We need you,"
said her sister and brother.
"You are the yellow in our daisy,"
said her aunts and uncles.
"And we are the petals,"
said all twelve of her cousins.
"Our family wouldn't be the same
without you," said her grandma
and grandpa.
"You are our little pizza pie,"
said her nonna and nonno.
"Assolutamente deliziosa!"
Rosie Roselli thought
about her Good Work,
the tempo in her toes,
and her bright red horn,
solid and snug in her backpack.
She thought about her family.
Maybe they do love me,
even when they can't
look or listen.

"Prove it," she said.

And they did.

Then Rosie Roselli rose up
on the toes of her saddle shoes.
She tried a little spin.
Her skirt spun out flat and round as a pizza pie.
Rosie bloomed.
She beamed.
For Rosie Roselli knew that
she was *assolutamente*
Rosie Fab-u-losa—

smack dab in the middle
of her heart.